T0381381

BoBo, my Favorite Teddy Bear!

Story and Illustrations By

Joyce Ann Landon

To order additional copies of this book, contact:
Xlibris
844-714-8691
www.Xlibris.com
Orders@Xlibris.com

ISBN: Softcover   978-1-4363-8097-3
         EBook   978-1-6641-8243-1

Print information available on the last page

Rev. date: 06/25/2021

Dedicated to my wonderful, adorable grandsons,

Jacob Jeffrey LeRoy

And

Alex James LeRoy

Here I am! I'm just one day old!

When I was just a little baby,
Grandma and Grandpa gave me
this brand new soft, fluffy Teddy Bear!

My new Teddy Bear is so-o-o, so-o-o, soft, clean, and fluffy!

I have all these animals in my crib!
They are all my friends and they are so much
fun to play with! Do you see the Teddy Bear
that Grandma and Grandpa gave me?
That's the one I really, really like!
It is so special!

This is Great Grandma! She loved holding us!
She wore a bright red, slippery coat!
We slid! Whee!

This is my uncle! He came from far away to see
me! He's big and strong! He held me real good!
Teddy Bear and I didn't fall!

Grandpa uses a wheelchair! Teddy Bear
and I like to ride on Grandpa's lap!
We ride all over the house!

I named my special Teddy Bear "BoBo"!

Mommy put me in the highchair with BoBo!
BoBo and I are eating peas! Uh-oh!
Some of the peas are on the floor!

I stand up now! I'm using my exercise toy!
BoBo and I press the buttons together and we
hear such funny loud sounds! Now Bobo and I
are spinning around and around and around!
What Fun! Uh Oh! There goes BoBo!

Uh Oh! BoBo is getting tired. Oh no!
BoBo is getting a little bit smudgy,
grungy, and is sort of.....shabby!
S-h-h-h! S-h-h-h! S-h-h-h!
Don't tell mommy and daddy!

Something real exciting just happened in
our family! Today mommy had a baby
at the hospital! BoBo and I are so, so, excited
to see the new baby!

BoBo and I get to hold the brand new baby! Little baby is so, so tiny! Look at the new baby's black hair!

BoBo and I snuggle close to daddy to look at our new baby! Having this baby in my house is going to be fun! BoBo thinks so too!

BoBo and I are in the big car seat in Grandma
and Grandpa's new car!
"Look at the big, red, truck!"

While mommy is at home taking care of our new baby, BoBo and I have a special day with Grandma and Grandpa! First, we stop at a restaurant for our breakfast! BoBo and I push this special kids chair right up to the table all by ourselves! Do you know what is really inside my "hamburger" sandwich? Why it's sausage and eggs! My favorite!

Our next stop is the library! We love
to go here! BoBo and I sit right on
Grandpa's lap! We love to ride Grandpa's
wheelchair right into the library!

That's my hand you see! When we go to the front door of the library, I always push this special button! It opens the door automatically for anyone who is handicapped! Grandpa, BoBo, and I go right in!

The first thing BoBo and I do when we are in the library is go to storytime! BoBo and I are sitting on the letter D on the bright blue storytime rug! I just love to listen to the stories! After storytime, all the children make a special craft! I take my craft home to my daddy, mommy, and my new baby!

The next thing BoBo and I do after storytime and craft, is go to the back of the library where the train sets are! We love to play with trains! BoBo watches me as I take the train around and around the table! I think it's lots of fun to play with trains, but at the library I always share them with others!

BoBo and I are done playing with trains for now! Next I find a great big library table and a big library chair! I pick out a great big kids book! I put it on the big library table and sit BoBo right beside me! I read the book to BoBo! I know BoBo really likes my story!

After we are finished at the library,
we go to the playground! Grandma swings me
way up high! I like to take BoBo
with me! Sometimes BoBo falls right out
of the swing! Uh Oh!

BoBo and I always have a fun day with Grandma and Grandpa! We always look forward to those special days! When I travel other places, I put BoBo in my backpack! Uh Oh! BoBo's head is sticking out of my backpack!

Well this is the end of my story about life
with my favorite Teddy Bear, BoBo!
I wonder how long I will keep BoBo with me? I'm
not old enough to go to school yet... but when
I get old enough I dream about taking BoBo to
school with me! I know what I would do! I would
put BoBo in my backpack but I would keep my
backpack closed so no one could see
BoBo hiding! That's what I would do!
It's time to go! Goodbye!

Printed in the United States
by Baker & Taylor Publisher Services